THE
MAGIC
TREE

a tale from the Congo

adapted and
illustrated by
Gerald McDermott

Holt, Rinehart and Winston
New York   Chicago   San Francisco

THE MAGIC TREE is adapted from an animated
film by Gerald McDermott produced by
LANDMARK PRODUCTIONS INCORPORATED

Published simultaneously in Canada by Holt, Rinehart
and Winston of Canada, Limited.
ISBN: 0-03-086716-9 (Trade)
ISBN: 0-03-086717-7 (HLE)
Library of Congress Catalog Card Number: 72-76567
Printed in the United States of America

First edition

Congo
River

for
Beverly

Time was,
there lived two brothers,
Luemba and Mavungu.

Born as twins,
they grew
and came to be
very different.

Their mother loved Luemba.
She smiled on him always.
She gave him fruit.

Mavungu was
given nothing.

One night he left his home.

Mavungu came to a place in the river.
A great tree was there,
so thick he could not pass.

When he pulled
the leaves
strange voices
spoke to him.

Mavungu was astonished.

From each leaf,
a new person.

Last to come
was a beautiful girl,
a princess.

She thanked Mavungu
for releasing her people
from The Magic Tree.
She vowed that
she would care for him.

She touched a charm
around her neck.
"I want to be his wife,
but he is so homely."
Again she touched the charm.
"I want to be his wife,
but he is in rags."

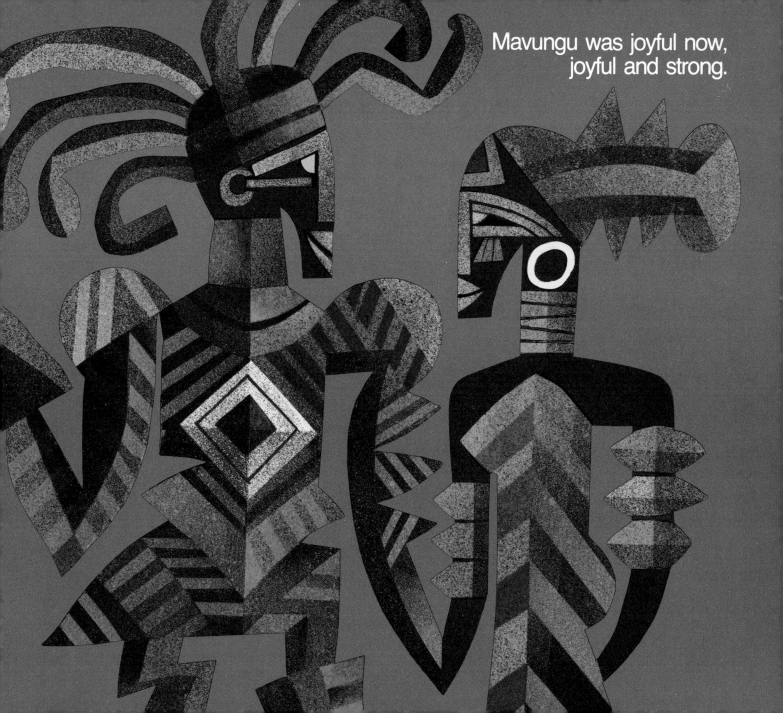

Mavungu was joyful now,
joyful and strong.

After a time, they passed near a wide place by the river.
The princess made a magnificent village grow up there.

Mavungu married the princess.
They exchanged vows of love.
But she pledged him to silence:
    The source of his wealth and pleasure must always be hidden.
    The secret of The Magic Tree must never be told.

The sun crossed the sky many times.
The moon grew to fullness.
And Mavungu thought of his family.

He sent for his mother
and his brother.
When they came,
he treated them kindly.

But his mother
wanted to know
Mavungu's secret.

He began to tell
of his journey down the river.
The princess stared at him.
His words became as silence.

The sun crossed the sky
many times again.
Once more
the moon grew to fullness.
Mavungu could not forget
his family.

Alone, he returned to his mother's home.

"Mavungu,"
said his mother.
"You left me long ago.
Tell me of your new life."

Mavungu forgot
his pledge of silence.
He forgot
those who loved him.
And he gave his secret to those
who did not love him at all.

"I wed
the princess
of The Magic Tree
and she made
a magnificent
village.

"I have been
very happy
there.

"Oh!"

ABOUT THE ARTIST

THE MAGIC TREE is Gerald McDermott's second picture book, based on a traditional African folktale. While the bold influence of African design is everywhere apparent in the book's presentation, much of its spontaneity also springs from the fact that it was first created as a film for young people.

In his youth, Gerald McDermott decided to become a graphic designer. His distinctive talent soon brought him attention and he won a Scholastic National Scholarship to New York's Pratt Institute. Upon graduation in 1964, the artist turned to his favorite medium and began to design, direct, and produce animated films. To date he has produced five films for young people, each of them a major award winner. Mr. McDermott's other activities include live-action films and television work.

Originally from Detroit, Michigan, the artist and his wife now divide their time between New York City and a home in southern France.

ABOUT THE BOOK

The artist designed this book and created the illustrations preseparated for color. The type face used throughout is Helvetica. The book was printed by offset.